1 3 5 7 9 10 8 6 4 2
ISBN: 978-0-00-758105-4
First published by HarperCollins *Children's Books* in 2014.

Text by Paddy Kempshall

Printed and bound in Italy

Visit www.tolkien.co.uk for news and exclusive offers!

If you have a smartphone, scan this QR code to take you directly to the Tolkien
website. You can download a free QR code reader from your app store.

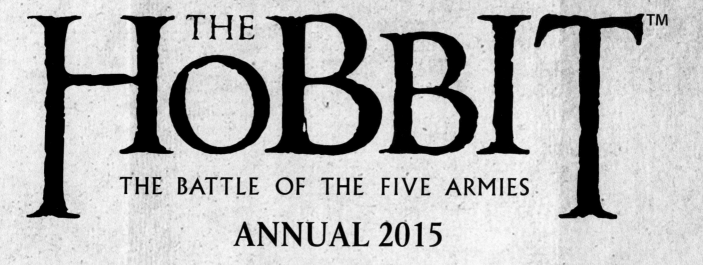

THE HOBBIT™

THE BATTLE OF THE FIVE ARMIES

ANNUAL 2015

HarperCollins *Children's Books*

CONTENTS

THE RACE OF MEN

Humans can be found in every corner of Middle-earth. In general, they are resourceful, resilient and brave. The Last Alliance of Men, led by the legendary Isildur, defeated the evil Sauron and helped bring peace to Middle-earth.

Time has not always been kind to the race of Men, and great kingdoms, such as the one at Dale near the Lonely Mountain, have long since been wiped from the face of Middle-earth.

Most of the Humans that Bilbo and the Company meet come from Lake-town. Built upon wooden stilts out on the waters of the Long Lake, it is a harsh place to live. The people there are poor, but proud, and live in hope that one day the Kingdom of Dale will rise again.

BARD

He would never seek out attention but Bard is a natural leader. That's no surprise, as he is actually the rightful last Lord of Dale! Bard is a cunning warrior and an expert archer – skills which he puts to great use once Bilbo and the Company come into his life and turn it upside down.

He has three children and cares deeply for them. He also cares for the rest of the people in Lake-town – he would think nothing of putting his own life in danger to save others.

THE MASTER OF LAKE-TOWN

While he might be the most powerful man in Lake-town, the Master is certainly not someone you would look up to. He may think that he is a man of taste and style, but the truth is he is dirty and rather ridiculous.

The Master is also very greedy and not just when it comes to food! He has quite an appetite for power and money, and he can't wait to get his hands on the share of Smaug's treasure which Thorin has promised to him.

His true nature isn't always clear to the people of Lake-town, but with Smaug heading towards the town, the Master's flaws may become obvious for all to see.

MASTER OF LAKE-TOWN

ALFRID

Alfrid is the Master's servant. He is also in charge of collecting all the taxes in Lake-town, which doesn't make him the most popular person around! While not truly evil, Alfrid is still not a very nice person. He takes great delight in using the small amount of power that he has to put himself above others and make their lives difficult.

He also cares more about saving his own skin than helping others and will go to great lengths to make sure that he survives – not always easy with a fire-breathing Dragon on his way to attack your home!

GRAND ADVENTURES

The path to Erebor has been a long and dangerous one for Bilbo and his companions. Read on and discover just how far from home Bilbo's adventures have taken him.

Bilbo has already travelled many miles from his home in the Shire. On his first night away he almost ended up as a Troll's dinner and things haven't improved very much from there!

After being chased by Orcs riding on Wargs; captured by Goblins; finding a magic ring, and almost being burned alive while clinging to a tree, he was only just past the Misty Mountains with many, many more miles of adventures ahead…

Rescued by some Giant Eagles, Bilbo, Thorin, Gandalf and the other Dwarves thought that they were safe – but Orcs don't give up that easily. Fleeing from the savage beasts, Gandalf led the Company to a strange cabin where they might seek shelter. But just as they were trying to get inside, a great roar shattered the air and they found themselves being chased by a huge bear-like creature instead!

The creature was called Beorn and it was his house the Company had found. A skin-changer, Beorn was a man who could change his shape. Luckily, he had no more love for Orcs than the Company, and eventually agreed to let Bilbo and his friends stay – they were safe at last.

Soon, however, Gandalf heard disturbing news that an evil Necromancer was lurking in the ancient ruins of Dol Guldur, far to the south. Realising that it was his duty to seek out the Necromancer, Gandalf was forced to leave the Company at the edges of Mirkwood.

As Bilbo and the Dwarves entered the dark, mysterious forest, Gandalf gave them a final piece of advice; on no account were they to stray from the Elven Road.

However, Mirkwood was a gloomy place, full of strange sounds and mysterious shadows and soon the Company were lost within its gloom. As the narrow path became darker, Bilbo and his friends suddenly found the way forward covered in strange, sticky webs! Without realising it, they had done exactly what Gandalf had warned them against: they had lost their way and wandered from the Elven Road…

Turn to page 24 to continue the adventure…

LAKE-TOWN ESCAPE

Smaug is on his way, set to devastate the town.
Can you help everyone get away before it's too late?

Puzzle 1: Help the Master get into the barge house and free a boat. To open the door you must link up all of the dots using only 4 straight lines and not taking your pencil off the paper!

• • •

• • •

• • •

Puzzle 2: Cross out all the letters below that appear more than once. Now use the letters that are left to discover from which direction Smaug will attack next, so you can avoid him.

D E Z R M
P C W O Z C A
S H B M T B D N
E W A C Z P S

Puzzle 3: You have 10 soldiers to help defend the town, but they have no swords. Which pile has the right number of swords to arm your soldiers? Decide quickly: Smaug approaches…

B.

C.

A.

Puzzle 4: Time to leave! Which path to take? The quickest path out of the town is the one with the smallest total when all of the numbers are added together.

A. 8 14 2 7 4
    10 6
B. 11 13 1 2 7
C. 6 6 9

THE WHITE COUNCIL

Middle-earth is a place of magic, both good and bad. To help keep the shadows of darkness at bay and to protect the world from evil, the White Council was created. Made up of some of the wisest and most powerful beings in the whole of Middle-earth, they are a formidable group.

Long ago, many Rings of Power were created and some are held by members of the White Council to help them in their task of protecting Middle-earth. One, Narya, is worn by Gandalf; another, Nenya, is worn by Galadriel and a third, Vilya, by Elrond. Of course, there is one ring which is more powerful than them all; and that is held by a dependable hobbit from the Shire.

The Council meets from time to time when great danger threatens Middle-earth. So when stories were heard of the Necromancer making his home in Dol Guldur, the Council sent Gandalf to investigate. However, he ended up finding more than he bargained for in those ancient ruins…

ELROND AND GALADRIEL

These are two of the most respected and powerful Elves in the land. Elrond is also known as the Elf Lord of Imladris and lives in Rivendell. A master of ancient languages, he discovered the hidden Moon Runes on Thorin's map which revealed the secret of the hidden entrance to Smaug's lair.

Galadriel, or the Lady of the Light, rules over the Lothlorien Elves. Beautiful and graceful, she is perhaps the most powerful Elf in Middle-earth. Particularly fond of Gandalf, she once even recommended that he be made head of the White Council.

GANDALF THE GREY

Gandalf is perhaps the most powerful wizard in all of Middle-earth. Old friends with the Elves (and also with quite a soft spot for hobbits), he has been alive much longer than any normal man.

Known to the Elves as Mithrandir (and to hobbits as someone who makes rather good fireworks), Gandalf is wise, powerful and cunning. It was Gandalf who brought Thorin the map and key to the secret entrance of the Lonely Mountain and helped start the whole quest. It was also him who recommended Bilbo as the burglar that the Company was missing!

RADAGAST

It's fair to say that if you were to meet Radagast you wouldn't think he was a powerful wizard at all. In fact you'd probably think he was a bit odd. It's not hard to see why when he spends all of his time in the woods talking to animals, and even has a sleigh that is pulled by a team of rabbits!

However, Radagast the Brown is indeed a powerful wizard. It was he who found the Morgul blade and alerted the Council to the dangerous happenings at Dol Guldur, and without his help things could have turned out very much worse for Middle-earth.

He may be a powerful wizard, but he's undeniably quite an odd one. Even his magical staff is a bit peculiar and sometimes doesn't work the way it should!

DID YOU KNOW?

Gandalf owns a magical sword called Glamdring which used to belong to an ancient and powerful king.

SMAUG AND HIS LAIR

For the past 170 years Smaug, has lurked in the darkness under the Lonely Mountain. Perched atop vast mountains of gold, he jealously guards his untold wealth.

Smaug is the last of the Dragons in Middle-earth. He is enormous, deadly, cunning and greedy. Thorin and his Company have their work cut out for them if they ever hope to defeat him. As if it isn't enough that he can breathe fire, or that his claws are the size of spears and his teeth like swords, Smaug's scaly hide is also so tough that normal weapons could never pierce it.

However, there is an old tale of when Smaug attacked Dale and was actually injured. During that attack he was shot with a fabled Black Arrow fired from a huge Dwarven weapon. Perhaps he is not as indestructible as everyone thinks?

Smaug is a fierce enemy with keen senses. While Smaug may be large, he can fly, and he's very quick for a creature of his size!

Greedy and corrupt, Smaug cannot stand the thought of anyone coming to steal the treasures he has collected. So when he discovers a small hobbit among his gold and gems he loses his temper in spectacular style.

DID YOU KNOW?

Just like Gollum, Smaug is also a big fan of games and riddles.

EREBOR AND DALE

"When the birds of old return to Erebor, the reign of the Beast will end." Such is the prophecy according to Oin, and it seems, now ravens have returned to the mountain, that the time has come.

Nearly 200 years ago, Thorin's grandfather, Thror, ruled over the Dwarven Kingdom in Erebor. For many years, the Dwarves had mined vast riches from under the mountain, including the Arkenstone. However, when Smaug heard of all the treasure, he attacked and scattered the Dwarves to the winds.

Smaug also destroyed the nearby city of Men, called Dale, and drove out the people there. The survivors went off to create Lake-town further to the south where they tried to survive by fishing and trading.

Now Thorin and his friends believe the time is right to return to the Lonely Mountain and take back their Kingdom. There's just the one small problem of having to get past the enormous dragon in order to do it!

TREASURE TRAIL

There are many tunnels and caves beneath the Lonely Mountain. Can you help Bilbo find his way through them to reach Smaug's gold? Try not to fall down any holes on the way!

START

FINISH

FOGGY FIGURES

Bard has lost his son in the thick blanket of fog which lies over everything. Look carefully and see if you can see the shadow that matches Bain.

A.

B.

C.

D.

E.

F.

G.

H.

BAIN

BARD

DOUBLE DRAGON

Smaug is the last Dragon in Middle-earth, but someone has cast a spell to make a copy of him!
Can you spot 8 differences between these pictures of the copy and the real Smaug?

UNDER FIRE!

Smaug is attacking Lake-town and burning everything in sight!
Can you help the Dwarves get the injured Kili to safety before it's too late?

START

1.

RULES

Find a counter (a coin is fine) and place it at the START.

Roll a die and move your counter along the board, following any instructions you land on.
If you roll a **1**, Smaug has burned another part of Lake-town and you must colour in one of the flames.

If you colour in all of the flames before you have reached the FINISH, Smaug has destroyed Lake-town before you can escape and you have failed!

If you want to play again, just draw your own flames on a piece of paper.

9. Go back to help find Bain, Sigrid and Tilda. Move back **1** space.

8.

7. You've lost your way in the smoke. Go back to the START and try to find your way again.

2.

3.

4.

5. KABOOM! A tower has collapsed in your way. Go back **1** space to find another path.

6.

10.

11.

12. Bard shows you a short-cut over the rooftops. Hurry on **2** more spaces.

13.

14.

15. Smaug has spotted you! Go back **1** space to find a place to hide.

16.

17.

18. You dodge Alfrid looking for helpers to load the Master's barge. Hurry on **1** space.

19.

20.

FINISH

GRAND ADVENTURES II

…continued from page 11

Before long, Bilbo and his friends realised that they were completely lost. Bilbo climbed a tree to see if he could spy a way out of the dark forest, but while he was looking, the Company was attacked by giant spiders!

Putting on his magic ring, Bilbo became invisible and began to fight the spiders. But even though he fought bravely, he could never slay them all as there were simply too many. Just as things were looking grim, a group of Wood Elves appeared, including the two mighty warriors Tauriel and Legolas. Launching into battle, they cut down the spiders, saving Thorin and the Dwarves.

However this turned out to be no rescue. Legolas and Tauriel led the Company to the fortress of Thranduil, the Elven King. Never one to let strangers wander in his land, Thranduil threw Thorin and the Dwarves into prison when they refused to tell him what they were doing in Mirkwood!

Luckily Bilbo was still invisible and had followed his friends into Thranduil's palace. While the Elves were drinking at a big party, Bilbo freed everyone and they managed to escape.

The Company weren't safe yet, though. As they were escaping, Kili's leg was badly wounded by a group of Orcs who had been tracking them. They were now caught between two groups of enemies who both wanted them dead!

However, the Elves started to battle the Orcs instead, and while they were busy fighting the Dwarves and Bilbo floated off down the river in some empty barrels to freedom. They landed on a deserted beach, but soon realised that they weren't alone, as a strange human with a deadly bow appeared out of the forest…

The Company managed to persuade the man, whose name was Bard, that they were merely merchants, and he agreed to take them with him to his home in Lake-town. But time was running out for the Company – they had only two more days to reach Erebor and open the hidden entrance to Smaug's lair.

Once they were safe in Bard's house, Thorin and the other Dwarves came up with a plan to continue their quest. The first thing to do was to find some new weapons. However, as Bilbo and his friends raided the town's armoury, Kili fell ill from the wound in his leg and the Dwarves were captured!

Dragged before the Master of Lake-town to hear their fate, Thorin promised him a share of Smaug's treasure in return for freedom. Thorin, Bilbo and the others were free once more, and just in the nick of time. For the next day was Durin's Day and their last chance to find a way into the mountain to complete their quest.

Turn to page 44 to continue the adventure…

LIFE AND DEATH

Kili the Dwarf has been injured, and his leg wound is life-threatening. Can you help Tauriel focus her healing powers on the wound before it's too late? Which is the correct path to Kili?

A.

B.

C.

DUNGEON DANGER

Gandalf has been imprisoned in the ruins of Dol Guldur.
Have you got the strength of mind to solve the puzzles and set him free?

Puzzle 1: The Orcs have laid a false trail. You need to make the arrow point in the opposite direction to show Gandalf's allies the correct path, but you only have time to move 2 pebbles! Which 2 pebbles will you move and where will you put them?

Orc trail:

Draw your answer here:

Move only 2 pebbles to make the arrow look like this.

Puzzle 2: Watch out! The path ahead is filled with traps. Use the secret key to help you work out a safe path through.

Secret Key: ᚠᛚᛚᛰᛗᛒᚠᛒᚠᛚᛚᛰᛗᛒᚠᛒ

START	ᚠ	ᛒ	ᚠ	ᛗ	ᛁ	ᛰ	ᛗ
ᛗ	ᛁ	ᛁ	ᛁ	ᛰ	ᛁ	ᛁ	ᛒ
ᚠ	ᛁ	ᛗ	ᛗ	ᛒ	ᚠ	ᛰ	ᚠ
ᛒ	ᛰ	ᛗ	ᛒ	ᚠ	ᚠ	ᛗ	ᛒ
ᚠ	ᚠ	ᛗ	ᛰ	ᛒ	ᛁ	ᚠ	ᛰ FINISH

Puzzle 3: Gandalf has left another clue, but it's in a riddle! Put the answer to each line of the riddle into the sum below to discover the Number of Power.

Riddle:

My first is in 14, but not in 4,

The next doubles 5 and not 1 more.

My third is the sum of 6 and 2,

The fourth is the number of me and you.

Sum:

$$(\underline{} \times \underline{}) + (\underline{} \times \underline{}) = ?$$

Puzzle 4: You have found Gandalf, but he is bound by magical chains! The weakest chains are those whose numbers add up to the Number of Power. Can you work out which chains to break and set Gandalf free?

Chain A. 1 11 4 7 9

Chain B. 4 2 10 8 2

Chain C. 5 8 1 7 5

Chain D. 7 4 9 3 7

Chain E. 1 6 3 5 9

Chain F. 9 2 6 4 5

THE RACE OF ELVES

Of all the peoples on Middle-earth, Elves are perhaps the most mystical and strange. Tall, slender and graceful, you wouldn't mistake an Elf for any other race.

Elves are not only one of the most magical races, they are also one of the oldest. In fact, Elves will never face 'the Doom of Men' as they are immortal and can live forever.

There are three main areas where Elves live: Rivendell, the Mirkwood and Lothlorien. Elves from each of these places are also different from each other. The Elves from Mirkwood, for instance, are shorter and have more obvious muscles.

Elves are fearsome warriors, especially known for their skills with a bow. Their swords and daggers are elegant and smoothly curved, sometimes looking more like works of art than weapons.

LEGOLAS

Although Bilbo and the Company don't know it when they meet him, Legolas is actually Thranduil's son. He is an expert with a bow, and perhaps the finest archer in all of Middle-earth. Unlike his father, Legolas truly wants to go out into the wider world and help to change it for the better. Indeed that is something that he will go on to do, having even more adventures with Bilbo and his family.

Legolas cares deeply for Tauriel and is torn between his feelings for her and his loyalty to his father.

TAURIEL

The head of the Elven Guard, Tauriel helps
to protect the kingdom of the Mirkwood Elves.
Her parents were killed by Orcs when she was
only a child, and she has a burning hatred for
their race. She is a highly-trained warrior and
is deadly at close quarters with her daggers.
Orcs had better run and hide when they
see her coming!

While Elves and Dwarves are not
traditionally the best of friends,
when Bilbo and his companions
arrive, Tauriel finds herself battling
some very odd feelings.

DID YOU KNOW?

The language of the Elves
is called Tengwar.

THRANDUIL

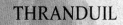

King of the Woodland Elves, Thranduil is cold and tough. Lurking
within his palace amongst the gloom of Mirkwood, he has no care for
the outside world and wants only to protect his own people.

Amongst the loot in Smaug's lair are some ancient Elven treasures
and Thranduil would do anything to get his hands on them again.

A fearsome warrior, he rides into battle atop an enormous elk, clad
in white armour and wielding a sword forged from a single sweeping
piece of metal.

MEMORY MATCH

Look at the picture below for two minutes (no peeping at the questions beneath it!).
Then cover it up and answer the questions to see how much you can remember.
Play with a friend to make it more competitive!

Player 1		Player 2
	1. How many characters are visible in the picture?	
	2. What is hanging in the top left corner?	
	3. What is Ori (the Dwarf with the white hair) holding?	
	4. Who is standing up?	
	5. How many cups are there on the table?	
	6. There are four windows in the picure. True or false?	

KINDRED SPIRITS

Middle-earth is filled with many wondrous races; have you ever wondered where *you* would fit into the world? Take this test and see which race you were born to be.

Your city is under attack and the people are called to arms. Which weapon will you choose?

A) I prefer to stay out of the thick of battle and use my keen eyes and reflexes to attack the enemy from afar. A bow is my choice.

B) Something functional and reliable, but effective – just like me. A sword is my weapon.

C) I don't care. Whatever I pick up from the nearest dead body. Or I might just use my teeth and claws…

D) What a foolish question! There's clearly only one weapon for a true warrior of bravery and strength. Bring me my axe!

You only have a day left to reach the secret entrance to Erebor before Durin's Day passes. What do you do?

A) It doesn't matter. I can wait for the next Durin's Day. It's only another year and I have all the time in the world.

B) Get a move on and do my best to get there in time.

C) Why would I want to go there? I'd rather be hunting on my Warg.

D) Gather a group of friends and hurry on. After smashing some things in a temper first, of course…

It's your birthday. What present would you most like to receive?

A) Something elegant and beautiful. Some art, or maybe a book of ancient wisdom.

B) A fine weapon, a cake and a party with my friends would be perfect.

C) The severed head of my enemy. And maybe their heart too.

D) Gold. Or gems. Silver's good too. Did I mention I like axes?

If you could have a best friend from all the other races on Middle-earth, what would they be?

A) Humans seem to have some wisdom and promise. Perhaps one of those would be an adequate choice.

B) I get on with pretty much anyone, but hobbits seem to know how to have a good time. They make me feel tall as well.

C) Something with the same lust for war as me. They'll need to like the dark and caves as well. A Goblin would do.

D) Anything except one of those arrogant Elves. They think they know everything. Plus they don't have beards. Never trust anyone who can't grow a fine beard.

You're having lunch when someone knocks into you and spills their drink all over you. What do you do?

A) When you've seen as much as I have you understand that these things happen. It's not important, so I'd forgive them. Anyway, I'm sure there's a spell which will clean it all up.

B) I'd be annoyed and have some words with them about being a bit more careful to look where they're going.

C) Rip their arms off so they couldn't ever carry a drink to spill again. Then I might eat one of their arms for good measure.

D) What a waste of good liquid! Did it go over my fine beard? If it did, then it's skull-cracking time. Otherwise it's fine – chainmail armour doesn't stain very easily…

YOUR RESULTS

 Mostly As: Elegant, wise, thoughtful and just a little bit magical. You'd fit right in amongst the Elves of Rivendell. Maybe you should start looking for some pointy ears to wear and learn how to use a bow?

 Mostly Bs: You would be one of the races of Men. Solid, dependable and sensible, you belong to one of the core peoples of Middle-earth on whom everything depends. Now the only choice is which area to live in!

Mostly Cs: Well, don't take this the wrong way and try to eat my head or anything, but you're an Orc. Which isn't a bad thing, you understand. Apparently serving an evil master and wanting to destroy everyone else shows great loyalty and focus…

 Mostly Ds: You're a Dwarf. Fierce, brave and just a little bit angry, you're quite the force to be reckoned with. You might have a slightly unhealthy love of axes and fine, bushy beards, but if anyone's ever in danger, they'd be wise to call on you for help.

LET THE BATTLE COMMENCE!

Choose your side and battle for control of the Lonely Mountain!

HOW TO PLAY:

1. Flip a coin to see who goes first.
2. The first player chooses one of their soldiers to use. Hold a pencil upright, placing the tip on the picture of the soldier you want to use.
3. Put one finger on top of the pencil and push down, firmly but not too hard.
4. Choose which of your enemy's soldiers to attack.
5. While still pushing down, slowly and carefully tilt the top of the pencil back, directly away from the soldier you're aiming at. WATCH OUT: when you have tilted it far enough, the pencil will suddenly slip and shoot away.
6. When the pencil slips, it will draw a line on the page. This is your attack.
7. If your line hits the picture of your opponent's soldier, that soldier is wounded and out of the battle.
8. Now it's your opponent's turn!
9. The winner is the person who wounds all of the other side's soldiers first.
10. Good luck!

BARD'S BOW

Bard is rushing to defend Lake-town from Smaug's attack, but he's unarmed!
Help him through the maze to find his bow and leap into action.

FINISH

START

TO ARMS!

An army of Orcs approaches! Help Thorin and the Company get ready for battle by finding the names of all their weapons in the grid below before it's too late.

The words can run up, down, diagonally and backwards too.

H	S	P	E	A	R	H	E	S	N	R	E	N	P	I	A
D	E	W	E	A	R	M	O	U	R	E	R	O	E	H	W
F	L	L	O	D	V	F	S	S	R	A	R	E	M	O	C
M	T	Z	M	C	E	A	W	A	H	P	O	F	R	T	N
P	A	A	I	E	D	E	A	A	F	A	N	R	N	H	S
L	S	A	R	H	T	B	T	T	R	E	A	S	N	N	N
E	I	T	I	O	S	E	K	O	D	H	E	T	U	S	M
N	T	T	A	N	S	T	O	R	C	R	O	P	O	B	R
H	L	M	A	F	W	N	B	C	E	O	O	R	E	N	M
A	E	N	A	E	F	A	O	H	L	G	M	N	N	N	H
E	T	T	L	D	T	G	E	I	L	L	G	A	R	Y	E
E	X	D	R	L	R	I	N	E	B	T	A	A	D	T	P
P	E	A	T	E	N	O	C	O	S	P	R	R	D	W	A
C	F	X	R	I	Q	S	W	O	R	D	Z	C	M	N	I
Y	R	L	W	H	O	S	A	N	I	W	N	T	D	E	R
A	H	W	M	S	W	E	R	N	A	N	A	T	P	R	R

BOW	SPEAR
ARROW	HELMET
SWORD	ARMOUR
AXE	WARHORN
SHIELD	TORCH
DAGGER	STAFF

STONE BUILDER

Thorin wants to protect Smaug's treasure from the approaching armies.
Draw a line to place the pieces of stone into the correct spaces to create some sturdy defences.

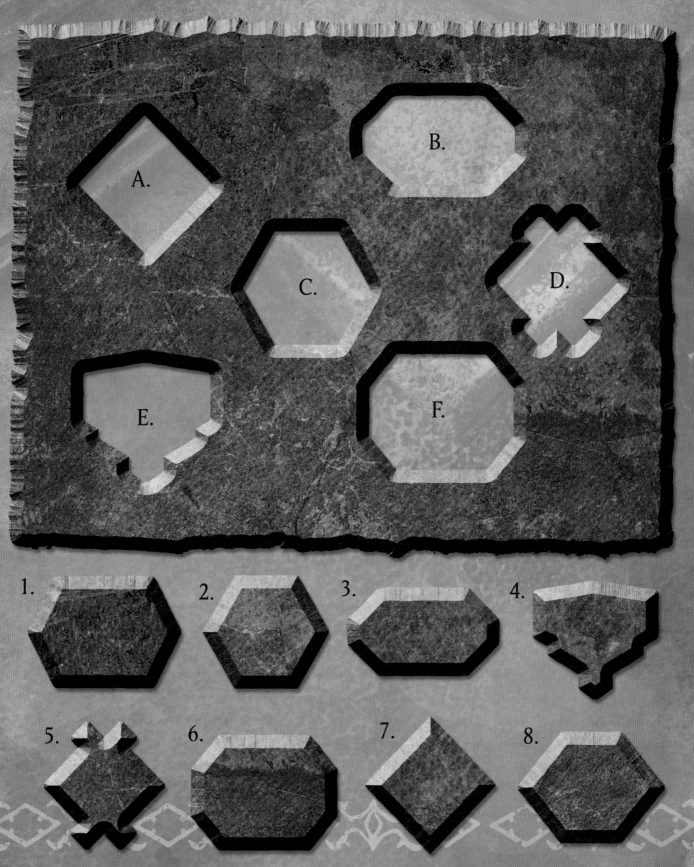

GOLD RUSH

With so much treasure in Smaug's cave, Thorin and the Company are going to need some help.
Put your smarts to the test and see if you're up to the task.

Puzzle 1: Balin has collected quite a sum of gold. But just how much?
Follow the number clues to work out how many gold pieces he has gathered.

The number of Dwarves in the Company

X

The number of Bard's children

−

The number of legs on a Warg

÷

The number of Kili's brothers

+

The number of years Smaug has been in Erebor

=

Total

Puzzle 2: Dwarves can be quite competitive and the race is on to see who can count the most treasure! Calculate the number at the top of each pile of gold to see who is the winner.

Pyramid 1:

21

| 8 | 13 | 12 | 9 | 6 |

Pyramid 2:

| 7 | 10 | 14 | 5 | 9 |

Pyramid 3:

| 8 | 12 | 11 | 16 | 13 |

Puzzle 3:

Bifur has found a very fine goblet, but now it seems to have gone missing. Lucky he labelled it with his name! Look carefully at the labels and see if you can work out which one is his.

A.   B.   C.   D.

A B C D E F G H I J K L M N O P Q R S T U V W X Y Z

Puzzle 4:

After all that counting Dori has dropped his gold! Look carefully at the pile and see if you can work out how many coins he has dropped.

Puzzle 5:

Deep amongst the treasure Nori has found a mysterious chest, but it's locked tight. Work out which symbols come next in the sequence to help Nori pick the lock and discover the riches inside.

43

GRAND ADVENTURES III

…continued from page 25

While Bilbo and his friends were continuing their quest, Gandalf was busy on his own adventure.
He had encountered the wizard Radagast at the High Fells, where they both discovered that an ancient enemy
was at work. Together they travelled to the ruins of Dol Guldur to investigate.

When they arrived, Gandalf gave Radagast a message to take back to the White Council and made him promise
not to follow him into the ruins.

Meanwhile, Bilbo and the Dwarves had travelled from Lake-town to the Lonely Mountain. Desperate to find the
entrance, the Company searched high and low for the door mentioned on the map. But to no avail. As the last
rays of sunlight faded, Thorin tossed aside the key and admitted defeat.

However, Bilbo wasn't so quick to give up. As he spotted the moon rising, he realised that the 'last light' of
Durin's Day was actually moonlight! Finding Thorin's key, he discovered the secret entrance and opened it wide.

All that remained now for the brave hobbit was to creep inside and steal the legendary Arkenstone gem from a
huge fire-breathing Dragon! Bilbo made his way past the largest piles of gold and gems that he had ever seen and
began his search.

But where to look amongst such a hoard of treasure? As he searched, Bilbo accidentally caused a landslide of coins; and uncovered the Dragon himself!

Remembering his ring, Bilbo slipped it on and became invisible. But he didn't realise just how clever Smaug was. Although the great Dragon wasn't able to see him, he could still smell him! Belching fire and fury, the Dragon chased Bilbo and his Dwarf companions through the caves, smashing walls and scattering treasure everywhere.

Somehow they managed to escape. In a rage, Smaug smashed his way out of the caves, blowing a huge hole in the side of the Lonely Mountain. Then, setting his sights on the city of Lake-town, Smaug set off to have his revenge…

Now Bilbo's adventure continues to its climax!

DOUBLE TAKE

**Bilbo has gone through many changes on his unexpected journey.
Can you spot 8 differences between these pictures of our unlikely hero?**

SHADOW SWORD

Bilbo has dropped Sting while searching Smaug's hoard and can't find it again amongst all that treasure. Look carefully at all the images and see if you can help Bilbo find his sword again.

A.　B.　C.　D.　E.　F.

G.　H.　I.　J.　K.

Sting

THE FORCES OF DARKNESS

When you know that there is a great fire-breathing Dragon to defeat at the end of your quest, it's hard to remember that Middle-earth is full of many other dangers too.

Once past the Misty Mountains, some of the greatest dangers to Bilbo and his companions, are Orcs.

If you were foolish enough to go looking for Orcs, then the fortress of Gundabad would be a good place to start. Far to the north of the Misty Mountains, it was an Orc stronghold, where they forged their weapons of war. It was thought that the Dwarves had destroyed Gundabad – though things are not always what they seem.

Orcs are related to Goblins, but are much larger and don't live underground. Like Goblins, they smell quite bad. They make their own weapons, but are happy to use anything that comes to hand to attack their enemies, including the weapons from fallen foes.

They are also known for their use of Wargs to ride in battle, as well as using slow-witted Trolls for all manner of things, including carrying catapults and battering rams.

Many in number and fearless, Orcs are the army of darkness and their task is to sweep the races of Man from the face of Middle-earth and bring their evil master to power.

BOLG

Bolg

Azog's son, Bolg, was sent by his father to pursue Thorin and the Company on their quest. After tracking them through Mirkwood, Bolg continued the chase, battling with the Woodland Elves as Bilbo and his friends made their escape.

However, the Company don't manage to shake Bolg that easily, and he continues to track them all the way to Lake-town.

AZOG

Also known as the Pale Orc, Azog is believed to come from Mount Gundabad. At around eight feet tall, Azog is a powerful figure and keen warrior.

During the battle of Azanulbizar, many years ago, it was Azog who killed Thorin's grandfather, Thror. During that same battle, Thorin also faced Azog and managed to cut off one of his arms! Thorin believed that he had wounded Azog so severely that he then died. However, reports of Azog's death were far from true.

Now the chief Orc in all of Middle-earth, Azog leads his forces as they seek to cast the land into darkness.

DID YOU KNOW?

No one really knows where Orcs came from, but some believe they are twisted and corrupted Elves.

HOARD HUNTER

There's so much treasure in Smaug's cave that the Dwarves don't know where to begin!
Draw a line to place each piece of the picture in the correct space to complete
the image and help the Dwarves to see all the dragon's hoard.

B.

A.

C.

D.

1.

E.

4.

5.

F.

G.

H.

I.

J.

2.

3.

6.

7.

THE RACE OF DWARVES

Short, hairy, loud and dangerous. That's what springs to mind when most people think about Dwarves.

Like Elves, Dwarves are an ancient race. They are expert miners and their Kingdoms used to be found under mountains across the land; from Khazad-dûm under the Misty Mountains, to Erebor. However over time the Dwarves have been driven from their homes, whether by Balrogs, Dragons or Orcs, and now find themselves a race in exile.

Dwarves are very passionate and upfront about how they feel, which can lead to lots of partying as well as lots of fighting! This might be one reason why Elves and Dwarves don't seem to get on very well and why Elves see Dwarves as a somewhat lesser race.

In battle, Dwarves are a force to be reckoned with. Preferring to use axes and hammers to most other weapons, they also use their blacksmithing skills to create magical armour from Mithril.

DWALIN

DWALIN

Dwalin is a tough, brave warrior with a reputation for speaking his mind and little time for fools – which, for him, is pretty much anyone who isn't a Dwarf. He has an aversion to Elves, like most Dwarves, though his feelings against them are even stronger than most. Fiercely loyal to his people and his King, Dwalin does not question Thorin's judgement – once you have earned his respect, this Dwarf would lay down his life for you.

KILI

Along with his brother, Fili, Kili has travelled far from his home in the Blue Mountains in search of adventure. Following his Uncle Thorin, Kili had little idea what he was letting himself in for!

Unusually for a Dwarf, Kili is an expert with a bow, although he is also very skilled with a number of other weapons. His weapon skills are not the only unusual thing about him though. For, while Thorin and many of the rest of the Company have a very Dwarvish reaction to meeting the Elves of Mirkwood, his feelings are not the same – especially when it comes to Tauriel…

THORIN

The son of Thrain and the last King under the Mountain, Thorin is the leader of the Company. His name translates as 'Darer' and he certainly lives up to it by setting out to try and kill Smaug and reclaim his family's treasure and kingdom.

While he may have set out with the best of intentions, sadly Thorin becomes more and more obsessed with the gold and other riches in Smaug's hoard – particularly the legendary Arkenstone. It is this greed that blinds Thorin to what is truly right and puts him and all of his friends in great danger.

DID YOU KNOW?

While they're not as bushy or full, female Dwarves have beards too!

While Men might use horses in battle, Dwarves are known to use armoured goats.

MAKE A MONSTER

Middle-earth is full of strange and deadly beasts, from vicious Wargs to a fire-breathing Dragon.
But what sort of creatures are lurking in your imagination? Get scary and design your own in the space below.

This is a _____

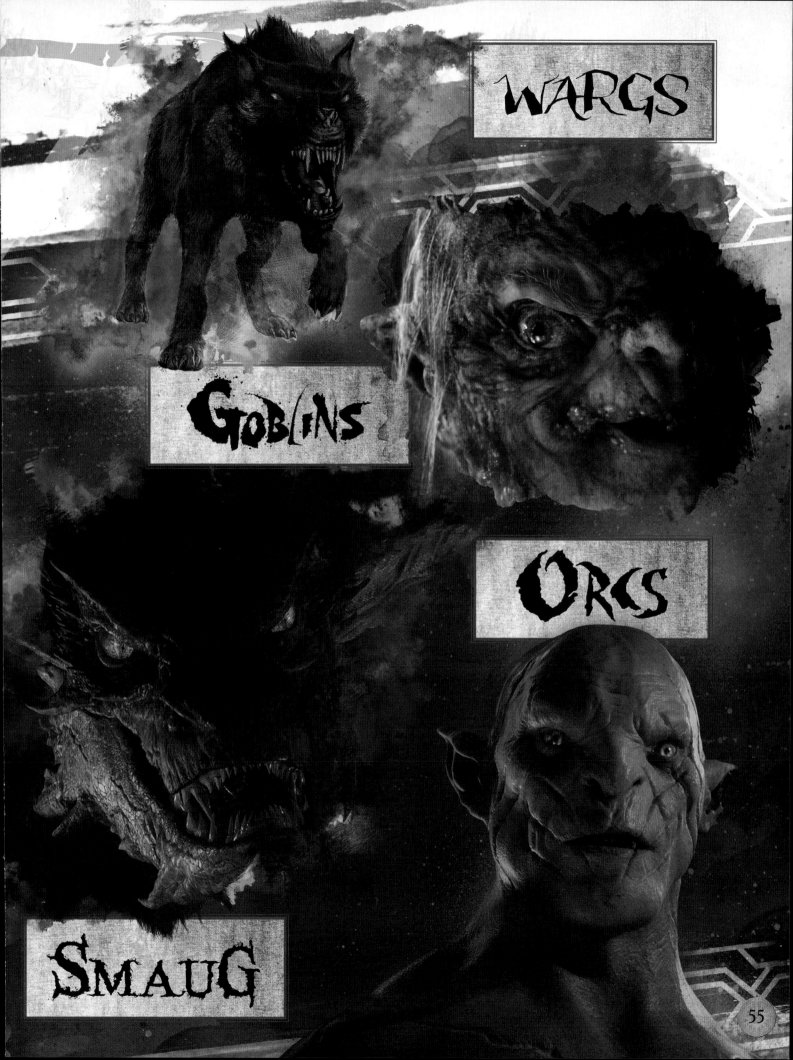

WARGS

GOBLINS

ORCS

SMAUG

CREATE A COMPANY

Now it's your turn to see if you can put together a team tough enough to take back Erebor.

With a friend, take turns drawing a line between two dots. If the line you draw completes a square, put your initials in it and score one point. Then take another turn. Look out for the bonus squares with people in to make your team stronger.

When all the dots have been joined up, the player with the most points has built the stronger team and is the winner!

Bilbo:	Double your whole score
Gandalf:	Add 4 points
Thorin:	Add 3 points
Kili:	Add 2 points
Dwalin:	Add 1 point

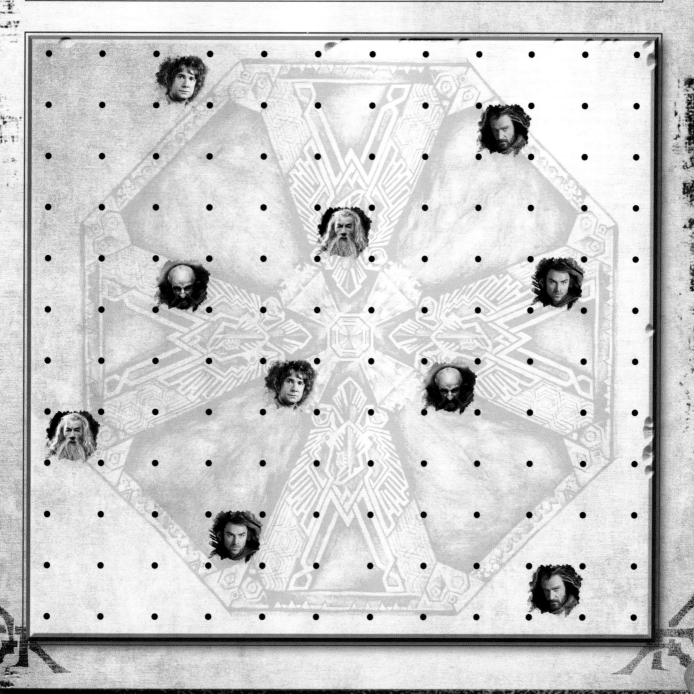

BRAIN BATTLE

It's been a long journey for Bilbo and his companions, filled with many adventures.
How much have you learned about the last part of their epic quest? Take this quiz and see.

QUESTION 1:
How many children does Bard have?

2, 3 or 4.

QUESTION 2:
What is the name of the jewel Thorin seeks above all others from Smaug's hoard?

Evenstar, Arkenstar, Arkenstone.

QUESTION 3:
For how many years has Smaug lived in the Lonely Mountain?

170 years, 1700 years, 17,000 years.

QUESTION 4:
Which race on Middle-earth speaks a language called Tengwar?

Dwarves, Orcs or Elves.

QUESTION 5:
Which agent of evil is this?

Azog or Bolg.

QUESTION 6:
True or False?

Another name for the Lonely Mountain is Erebor.

[ ]

QUESTION 7:
What is the name of the skin-changer who can turn into a bear?

Bard, Balin or Beorn.

[ ]

QUESTION 8:
What is the name of Kili's brother?

Bili, Fili, or Sili.

[ ]

QUESTION 9:
Which of these is not a traditional home of Dwarves?

Gundabad, Khazad-dûm or Erebor.

[ ]

QUESTION 10:
True or False?

There is another Dragon rumoured to be living in the ruins of Dol Guldur.

[ ]

ANSWERS

pages 12-13
LAKETOWN ESCAPE
Puzzle 1:

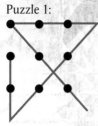

Puzzle 2: N O R T H
Puzzle 3: C
Puzzle 4: Path B: 10, 2, 1, 6, 9 (total 28)

pages 18-19
TREASURE TRAIL

page 20
FOGGY FIGURES
Shadow F

page 21
DOUBLE DRAGON

page 26
LIFE AND DEATH

pages 28-29
DUNGEON DANGER
Puzzle 1:

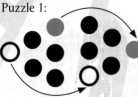

Puzzle 2:

START	ᚠ	ᛒ	ᚠ	ᛗ	ᛁ	ᛉ	ᛗ
ᛗ	ᛁ	ᛁ	ᛚ	ᛁ	ᛚ	ᛁ	ᛒ
ᚠ	ᛁ	ᛗ	ᛗ	ᛒ	ᚠ	ᛉ	ᚠ
ᛒ	ᛉ	ᛗ	ᛒ	ᚠ	ᛗ	ᛗ	ᛒ
ᚠ	ᛚ	ᛗ	ᛉ	ᛒ	ᛁ	ᛉ	FINISH

Puzzle 3: Solution: (1x 10) + (8x 2) = 26
Puzzle 3: Solution: Chains B, C and F

page 32
MEMORY MATCH
1. 10
2. lamp
3. bow
4. Bard
5. 3
6. False

page 38
BARD'S BOW

page 40
TO ARMS!

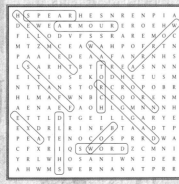

page 41
STONE BUILDER
A=7, B=3, C=2, D=5, E=4, F=6.

pages 42-43
GOLD RUSH
Puzzle 1:
12 (Dwarves) x 3 (children)
− 4 (legs) ÷ 1 (brother) +
170 (years) = 202 pieces of gold!

Puzzle 2:

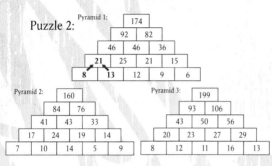

Puzzle 3: Label C.
Puzzle 4: 31 coins
Puzzle 5: red square, blue triangle

page 46
DOUBLE TAKE

page 47
SHADOW SWORD
Sting =I

pages 50-51
HOARD HUNTER
1=D, 2=I, 3=H, 4=C, 5=A, 6=E, 7=G.

pages 58-59
BRAIN BATTLE
1. 3
2. Arkenstone
3. 170
4. Elves
5. Azog
6. True
7. Beorn
8. Fili
9. Gundabad
10. False. Smaug is the last Dragon in Middle-earth.